# The
# Coin

SARAH HART

First ebook edition: April 2013
First paperback edition: April 2013

The Coin: a novella by Sarah Hart
Cover design: Go Bold Designs by Cory Clubb—
coryclubb.com

ISBN: 0989296105
ISBN-13: 978-0-9892961-0-6

# DEDICATION

To my husband and to my parents. Thank you for your
support and for always believing in me.

# CONTENTS

# ACKNOWLEDGMENTS

Mom, you were the first person that saw my interest in writing and encouraged it. Dad, you gave me advice and support, and both of you gave me the creative gene, so thank you very much. You helped turn my dream of publication into reality. Greg, you pushed me past my comfort zone and always asked me 'why not' when I tried to give an excuse as to why this story wasn't ready for the public eye. You are heaven sent and mean the world to me.

I need to recognize and thank God. His inspiration flowed through my hands as this story came to life. He is the reason it exists at all. My hope is that *The Coin* inspires love and forgiveness, both for ourselves and for others. Life is about learning and growing. Let's work at making this world infused with love. It could always use more.

# The
# Coin

# 1. CHRISTMAS EVE

"Tara, *wake up*!" My mother's voice rang quietly but shrilly in my ear, waking me up from what had promised to be a good nap.

I opened my eyes unwillingly, staring with sleep-blurred vision at the scene before me: I was in church, and some guy was *still* droning on about how appropriate it was to spend Christmas Eve in God's house, reflecting on Christ and his birth.

*Boring!*

I closed my eyes and grumbled, "Mom, don't wake me up until church is over."

I slunk down lower against the bench, but my mother grabbed onto my arm tightly and yanked me back up. I glared at her and twisted my arm angrily out of her grip.

"It's Christmas Eve, can't you listen for one day out of the year, young lady?" she whispered with weary exasperation, her hazel eyes pleading with me to cooperate.

I crossed my arms. "Can't listen when my ears fell off from the most boring crockpot story of the century!" I hissed quietly in retort.

Private satisfaction fluttered away inside of me as my mother's eyes widened with stunned shock.

Take *that*.

My mother was a spiritual woman who, along with my dad, was raising my younger brother Shawn and me to be good Christian people. We went to church and read from the scriptures and said prayers and talked about God and Jesus. We helped out our neighbors and sometimes volunteered with community cleanup projects. That was all well and good, but sitting in church hearing a boring story that I'd heard a million times about a guy who came to save us from our sins? I wasn't buying it anymore. My friend Jessica and I decided Jesus was just a story parents told their kids so they would behave and think someone other than mom and dad was watching them. As a fifteen year old, that kind of stuff was just getting *old* by now. Didn't Mom get that?

Judging by the sadness creeping into her eyes, I guessed that the idea was finally beginning to sink in. I pushed away the twinge of guilt that stabbed at my heart. Jessica thought that when a parent looked at you like that, it was the most important time to stand up for yourself, or you'd never be taken seriously. I agree, so I lifted my chin high and met my mother's eyes with grim determination.

"This is Christmas, Tara," my mother began, her whispered voice pleading with me to take back my words. "*Christ* is the reason we celebrate this season at all! You know that. You've always known that."

I rolled my eyes and snorted softly. "Yeah, the season celebrates Santa Claus too, and look how real *he* turned out to be."

My mother's mouth dropped slightly. Her brows furrowed, and she frowned with a knowing expression. "It's that Jessica girl, isn't it?" Her head shook sadly. "I wish you wouldn't listen to the things she says."

My jaw clenched as I ground out the words, "I *like* Jessica! She tells me how things really are!"

Mom opened her mouth, a counter argument on the tip of her tongue, when she cast a glance behind her at the crowded room of eyes staring forward at the speaker and clicked her mouth shut.

"We'll talk about this later," she muttered through tight lips, leaning in close.

I hid my smile. There was no doubt my mom would try to talk about this later—a conversation I was already prepared to do my utmost to avoid—but for this small moment in time, I had won the argument, and that felt good.

For the remainder of church I didn't slouch or fall back to sleep, but I also didn't try to stifle the yawns or the impatient sigh, silently reveling in the stern looks my mother threw my way and how her lips pursed together, straining to hold back words that weren't reverent enough for a crowded room on Christmas Eve.

When we got home, I immediately latched onto Shawn and involved myself in a game of 'Guess Who.' I stuffed down the guilt that arose when his confusion turned into radiant delight that I had decided to not only spend time with him, but to spend *hours* with him—something I hardly ever did anymore because hanging out with my ten year old brother was just so boring. However, today he served my purposes well in avoiding the conversation I knew was boiling on my mother's tongue.

When we were putting on our winter coats to head outside, my dad had that disappointed gleam in his eye when he asked to speak privately with me for a moment. Knowing full well that Mom must have spoken with him, I dived underneath his arm and pelted Shawn with a sloppy wad of snow. Shawn laughed and threw one that totally smacked me in the head. For a moment my mask slipped and I wanted to wipe that smile clear off my brother's face, but my parents were watching and so I laughed instead, engaging a snowball fight that lasted long enough for our noses to turn into bright pink buttons and our hands and feet to grow so numb we had to help each other peel our layers of sodden winter clothing away.

By that point, the familiar magic of Christmas Eve had settled into the house, and I had nearly forgotten that Shawn was my annoying younger brother. He was on my temporary list of cool little dudes, and we talked excitedly about the Christmas presents we hoped to receive and the food we were eager to eat.

The morning's friction between my mother and me had been laid to rest and—though not forgotten—had been put on the back burner. We ate our traditional home made pizza that was customary to make on Christmas Eve and Mom grumbled about us eating too many of the pepperoni before it made it into the oven.

As also was our tradition, we sat down and watched Albert Finney's version of 'Scrooge' and sang along to the music, quoting our favorite lines and laughing as we tried our failing best to imitate the Cockney English accent of the choir boys. I ignored the pointed looks from Mom as Ebenezer found himself transformed from his crabby, selfish ways into a man who held the true spirit of Christmas.

It wasn't until bedtime came around when Mom tried to get us to say what our favorite story of Jesus was that the pleasant little family bubble popped for me. Shawn had been more than willing to share that he had so many favorite stories that it was hard to pick just one—the mewling little brat—but when it came time for me to spill my non-existent guts, I simply refused. I threw my arms up in the air.

"This is stupid!" I yelled out and stalked off to my bedroom, ignoring my parents calling after me.

A moment later Shawn tried to come into my bedroom to soothe me, emboldened by the day's camaraderie between us. I snarled at him and pushed him out, ignoring the guilt that arose when his face fell into confused hurt. I locked my bedroom door and threw myself down on my bed, arms crossed and huffing with righteous indignation that was my due right to feel as a teenager.

I didn't want or need anybody to cheer me up and tell me about Christ. He was a good bed time story, and that was it. The sooner my family got that, the better.

I expected to hear insistent knocking from my parents, demanding to come in and talk to me, but the sounds never came. I lay on my bed, curled up and left alone in peace.

Good.

## 2. THE DREAM

The sounds of the house grew quiet, and after a time I drifted off to sleep. At first I dreamt of Christmas and the loads of presents I had received and the happy smiles on my parents' faces, but then they swirled out of focus and fights with my mother surfaced as well as Shawn's hurt, angry face when I shoved him away before bed.

I tossed and turned with restless agitation until those dreams melted away and became something entirely different. There was a shift, and a new dream surfaced that I would never, ever forget: A dream that taught me a greater meaning, and changed me forever.

I found myself on a cobblestone road in the dark of night. My bare feet plodded along, rubbing against the dirt that dusted the path, feeling the rough texture of the uneven stones. There was the faintest trace of heat that radiated from them, dispelling the last of the sun's warmth it had gathered throughout the day. The night air whispered against my skin, caressing it as a warm breeze combed through my tousled hair. There was a slight chill, but it never reached my bones.

I looked up and beheld a million stars that glimmered and sparkled, stretching across a huge span of sky. I felt my jaw open in wonderment, and I looked down to take in the rest of my surroundings. Even though it was a black night with no other light than the stars and moon in the sky, I had no troubles seeing through the darkness.

Some part of my subconscious knew that I was dreaming, knew that this wasn't real, but my mind grappled with a profound sense that all of this was *very* real. The earthy scent of dirt wafted to my nose as it kicked up under my feet. Never before in any of my dreams were all of my senses turned on as they were now. I pinched myself out of curiosity; yup, that hurt.

Weird!

Taking in my surroundings, I noticed the road I stood on took me to a wrought iron gate leading into a garden full of trees; I could almost smell the fresh grass and floral aroma. Beside the gate on each side were two men slumped over, deep in slumber. Their apparel was strange: they wore long earth-tone robes of cotton with a second layer slung up and over them like a sash. They had long beards and wore thin sandals on their feet. They reminded me of people from olden time— *very* olden time.

Something inside urged me to walk forward, past the slumbering men and into the garden, an invisible string pulling me along as I wandered down a dirt path, feeling small pebbles wiggle between my toes. I stopped for a moment, closing my eyes and inhaling the strong floral scent of begonias and geraniums that filled the air when a man's loud wailing wrapped its tormented grip around my heart, alerting me to deep sorrow nearby. His cry came from somewhere within the garden, the sound drawing me to find his location. I *knew* that voice. How did I know that voice? Why, oh why did it sound like it was breaking into a million fractured pieces?

In a frenzy I followed those despairing cries, feeling a thorn of sorrow pierce into my heart the closer I got to the source. I had to find this man, find the person my heart was bleeding for, would gladly bleed for if it meant that agonizing sound could end. I stumbled through the thicket of trees, coming closer, until . . .

I saw him.

He was kneeling over a very crooked and bent tree, his face pressed against the gnarled bark, his long sweat-soaked golden brown hair hiding his face from view. Those cries of agony had stopped and he was breathing heavily, his robes of exquisite white stained and covered with sweat and. . . was that blood? His hands clenched to the knots of the tree as if his life depended on it, those fingers gripping with a fierceness I felt bruising into my bleeding heart.

Everything inside of me ached at the world of agony this man was locked into, giving no indication he had heard me approach. I watched his back rise and fall in great shuddering, heaving breaths.

I wanted to run up to him, but my feet wouldn't give.  Something inside prevented me from rescuing this man from the torment I beheld.  My knees felt weak and threatened to fall out from beneath me, but somehow I managed to hold my ground, willing the thorns that pierced my heart to ease and give me strength to draw air and speak.

"W-What's wrong?" I managed to croak out.

The man took a shuddering breath, never looking up.  "You have forgotten me," he sobbed.

"I—what?" I asked, surprised by his response and the deep sorrow in his voice I was grappling to understand.

"You have forgotten me," he repeated, bringing his head up, though his hair still hid his features from view.

Sudden fire flared in my beating heart, telling me something that my mind wasn't hearing.  What did he mean?  He did *look* familiar, but why wasn't I recognizing him?

My breathing became ragged as I struggled to find a response.  "I—I'm afraid I don't understand," I found myself saying.

"I came into the world, and mine own received me not," he replied woefully, lifting his head so his dampened hair fell away, revealing eyes that looked into mine with heart breaking sadness.

9

I let out a gasp.

Those *eyes*.

I knew those eyes. With startling clarity that crashed into my chest with earth shattering force, I realized I knew that man.

He was Jesus the Christ.

Tears sprung to my eyes. *No.* No! "Nooo!"

Did I say that out loud? Did he say I'd forgotten him? I shook my head in dumbfounded apprehension. "No! I—I didn't, I would never—" forget you.

The words died in my mouth, because suddenly, as much as I wanted to say them and erase the pain from his eyes and soul, I knew they weren't true.

Too many images came unbidden to my mind of all the instances in my life where I made the choice to forget about Christ. I turned my back on who He was, who He became, and who He wanted me to be. I listened to other people instead, chose to. . . oh, all the things I *chose* to do!

I don't remember falling to the ground in a sobbing heap, guilt slashing away at all of the memories that flew before my mind's eye. *So* many times I chose to forget about Him, to exclude Him from my life, and now here He was, right in front of me. He was paying for my negligence. Paying with blood and sweat and tears—so many tears!—for everything my teenage rage thought was unfair. How could I face the man in front of me? How could I possibly have the proper words to tell Him I had realized, *too* late, how much I had hurt Him?

I don't know when His hands found their way to mine, but I do remember the warmth and the love that spread from them and travelled up and into my heart. I don't remember Him placing anything into my hands, but I do remember the marred gold coin that illuminated in my palm when it opened up to reveal the object that was suddenly there. I remember the instant peace that settled over my fragmented soul as I beheld its wonder. The edges weren't quite smooth, it looked worn and well handled with indentations in the precious metal, but there were no other markings to distinguish the coin's currency.

Rough but gentle fingers tilted my chin upward, gently coaxing my eyes to look back into those crystal clear depths. I expected to see the terrible pang of grief and sorrow in those deep pools of color, but instead I saw Christ's eyes looking at me with such open, unabashed brotherly love. I felt the air leave my lungs as the depth of such strong emotion flowed through me.

The corners of His mouth lifted up as He spoke softly, "This is my gift to you." He slowly closed His hand around mine. I felt the coin wrapped inside my palm, radiating with a heat that seared into my soul and yet did not burn. "I paid for your sins of my own free will," Jesus continued, His soft words etching into the very fiber of my being. "I partook of the bitter cup, and overcame the world. I did it for *you*. I will never forsake you. Please," He implored, those stunning eyes burning into mine, "do not forsake *me*."

Tears pooled in His magnificent eyes. Tears of compassion and strength and forgiveness and – above all, love. So much love, beyond count, beyond measure, beyond time. For me.

For *me*.

Wracking sobs of grief washed over me again. How could He love me after all that I'd done? He'd said I'd forgotten him, and I *had*. How could He . . . how could He . . .

"I—I," I stammered among my sobbing. "I am *so* sorry," I wailed. "I didn't mean to hurt you. I let myself forget you and I shouldn't have done that, how can you . . ."

Forgive me. I wanted to ask it, but the words didn't make it out of my mouth. Looking in His eyes, *feeling* that love wash over me, I realized that my question had—with astounding force—already been answered. Jesus had not only forgiven me, but—I rubbed at the coin he'd pressed into my hand—He had paid for the opportunity for me to start over. I *could* start over. I could go forth and remember Him. I *could* go forth and serve Him.

Suddenly my tears of grief turned to tears of overwhelming joy, and my body shook anew with fresh, overflowing emotion. Jesus gathered me in His arms, saying nothing, and yet saying everything. I felt His strong arms wrap around me, and I melted in His embrace.

"Remember me always, and the sacrifice I made for you."

I wasn't sure if those words were actually spoken out loud, or if they were words He spoke into my heart, but all the same I nodded my head and gave a shuddering "I *will* remember" as I wrapped my arms around Him as tight as I could hold, continuing to sob from the endearing love that was flowing through me.

# 3. AFTERWARD

When I opened my eyes, I realized that I was in my own room, hugging the life out of my pillow. Dazed, I sat up in bed and wiped the tears away from my face, blinking in confusion.

I was wide awake. It felt like I had been awake for a very, very long time. I was back in my own room, and a glance at the clock told me it was six forty five in the morning.

That had all been a dream?

I shook my head. It had felt so real, and yet . . . dreams weren't anything more than just my imagination . . . right? Pain stabbed at my heart; why did it have to end? I would have stayed in that embrace for ever and ever.

Sighing, I slung my legs up and out of bed. It was Christmas Day. Heading for my door, I opened it and stepped back as my stocking fell onto the floor, some of its contents spilling out. It was tradition in my home to wake up with the stockings at the foot of our door. Bending down, I dug through the stocking with half-hearted enthusiasm, my mind still too full from my dream when something shiny caught my eye. Focusing my attention, I let out a gasp when I realized what it was I had picked out from my stocking: the marred golden coin, the very one from my dream.

I stared with wide-eyed wonder—how?

The shiver that coursed through me, speaking to my heart and to my soul, told me the answer to that question didn't matter. I knew how—Christ. This was His gift to me, His token, His reminder.

Fresh tears brewed in my eyes as I closed my hand around the coin, feeling it as I had only moments before.

"I *will* remember you," I whispered softly into thin air.

A warm blanket of love wrapped itself around my heart in answer.

Smiling with giddiness and bursting at the seam, I quickly pulled on my robe and ran into Shawn's room without knocking. I jumped onto his bed and threw my arms around my sleep-sodden brother.

"Merry Christmas! You're the coolest dude I could ask for in a brother." I ruffled his hair and gave him a wet kiss on the cheek.

"Aw, gross!" Shawn wiped away at it, rubbing his

hand next against his bed sheets to fully expel my cooties from his skin. He looked at me with wary, questioning eyes, trying to gauge if this was just Christmas talk or if I actually meant what I said.

Last night's tantrum flashed through my mind.

"I'm sorry I've been a jerky sister lately," I apologized, putting my arm around him. He didn't try to pull away. "I promise, from this point on, I'll be a better older sister for you. We'll hang out more often. Yesterday was fun." I flashed him a bright smile, and Shawn slowly returned it.

"Yeah, it was," he agreed. "I totally threw more snowballs than you!"

I laughed and ruffled his hair, giving him a playful shove before jumping off the bed as he pushed my arms away.

"Let's go wake up Mom and Dad."

Shawn eagerly got out of bed, pausing at the door when he saw his stocking. I waited patiently while he rummaged through it, thinking idly that he wasn't such a bad brother after all. I just needed to give him more of a chance, something Mom always harped on me about. Well, she didn't need to harp on me anymore.

"Come on, Shawn!" I urged him.

Shoving the contents back into his stocking, he scooped it into his arms and walked with me toward our parents' bedroom as we eagerly pounded on their door and heard the muffled groans of 'we'll meet you down by the tree. Don't open anything yet!'

Shawn and I raced down the hallway and into the living room, our eyes taking in the feast before us. Shawn raced over and started to find which gifts belonged to him, but I hung back, fingering the coin I kept in the pocket of my robe.

I'd already been given the best gift I could have asked for, and when my parents came down to join us, I was going to give them the best present they had ever received from me in years— Love.

# ABOUT THE AUTHOR

Sarah Hart lives with her husband and furry Lionhead bunny child in Utah. This is her first published work, though it will not be the last. She has a love of writing, spending time with her husband, soul searching, and Disneyland. She believes that Jesus Christ and Mickey Mouse have a good thing going.

You can find her musings at
www.booksbysmiles.blogspot.com
You can also find an ebook version of *The Coin* for Kindle at Amazon.com